A GREEK SUMMER

Patricia Frew

Michael Terence
Publishing

First published in paperback by
Michael Terence Publishing in 2018
www.mtp.agency

ISBN 9781912639014

A GREEK SUMMER

Patricia Frew

The sun shines once again, it's spring
Air redolent with scents of herbs
Water in the bay a shimmering blue
White fluffs of clouds meander o'er the sky
Wild cyclamen appear from every crack
Daisies raise their faces to the sun
For a few short weeks our island will be green
Before the long hot summer takes a hold

The almond blossom's heavy on the trees
The sounds of bleating lambs to make one smile
Warm sun touches winter skin
Foretaste of summer heat to come
Blue sky, washing blowing in the breeze
Children playing football in the square
Our island waking up from winter sleep
Uplifts the soul, so pleased to be alive

Tourists flock here for relentless sun
To lie on beaches broiling, turning red
Thinking they know the island very well
But never glimpse it as it is right now
They see it brown and scorched with heat
A harsh and craggy rock arising from the sea
They never breathe this green and lovely isle
A tiny part of Greece that is my home

A Greek Summer

Towards the end of the season I found Manolis leaning thoughtfully on the bar slowly wiping non-existent stains on the counter.

Everyone passed through the hotel at some point. Both locals and tourists alike and Manolis saw it all.

He missed nothing. He noticed who was with whom, holiday romances and local affairs alike.

Not in a nasty way you understand but only because he was interested in all human life and was genuinely fond of all of his customers with only the odd exception.

He ran the hotel together with his wife and son but Manolis liked to be front of house and get to know his guests and chat with them in the bar.

The hotel was just around the corner from the main harbour and had amazing views across the water. Each room had its own balcony and en-suite and although not the Ritz it was clean, comfortable and welcoming.

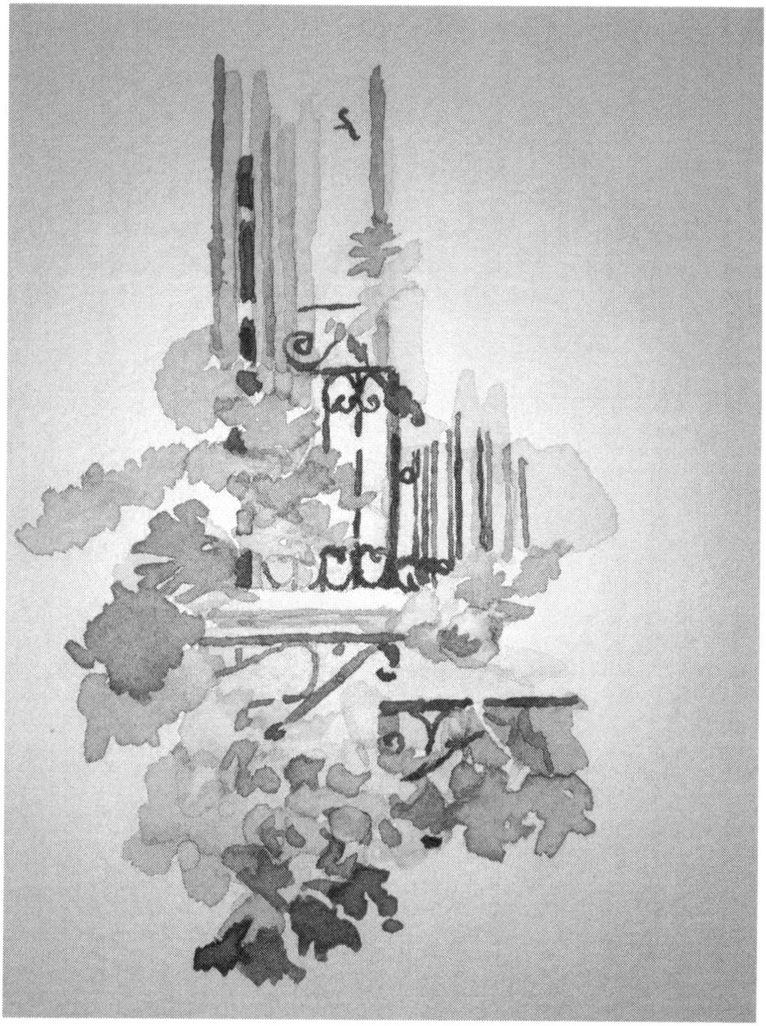

The reception and bar area was spacious and airy. On the left stood a waist-high dark wood counter with pigeon holes behind. This served as the reception. Tucked away under a magnificent wooden staircase was an extremely well-stocked bar. The whole area smelled of wax polish.

There were a few low tables and comfortable chairs but the majority of people chose to sit out by the water where the chairs were not so comfortable and the tables sometimes less than steady but the breeze from the sea and the wonderful view made it all worthwhile.

"Ah . . . *filo mou* . . . when did you get back? Come and sit with me by the water and have a drink."

We hugged each other. We southern Europeans are more touchy-feely than our standoffish neighbours in the north. We hug our children and hug our friends both male and female.

Manolis poured the drinks and we carried them out to a table by the sea. We settled in a couple of well-used chairs and Manolis wedged a beer mat under the table leg to steady it.

Although it was October it was a balmy evening. The water lapped in the slight breeze and the setting sun cast a panoply of colours on to the distant Turkish mountains.

The air of my beloved island caressed my skin and the

atmosphere was fragrant with the scent of wild herbs.

The cicadas whirred noisily in the nearby trees and the slow clang of goat bells came from the hills as the animals foraged for scarce food. Soon the rains would come and the dry dusty ground would come alive and the grazing would be thick and succulent again.

“I see you’re still smoking as much,” I said as Manolis shook a cigarette from the packet and flicked a plastic lighter.

“And you’re still smoking that filthy pipe.”

I have always loved my pipe. The whole routine of filling it, tamping it down and the repeated attempts to light it with match after match fill me with a simple pleasure. I can fill an ashtray with spent matches before ever getting a decent draw.

So we sat in silence for a while; two old friends smoking and relaxed in each other’s company.

We were both past our prime. Pushing sixty if truth be told but in our heads we were still the young boys who had played together, played truant from school together and chatted up the girls. Our ways had parted in our twenties when I chose to go off to sea and Manolis eventually took over the hotel from his ageing parents.

"So... .has it been a good season for you?"

“Very good my friend; we’ve had a fine mixture of people both staying here and dropping in. You remember even the locals use the bar. They know I’ll not charge them the tourist prices and they know that I always know what’s going on so we have a give and take of island news.”

“You mean gossip,” I laughed. “Anyway tell me about who was here and who’s doing what and to whom.”

"Well, we were all delighted when Yannis met his English lady Maria. You remember his first wife... .what a bitch. She led him a merry dance and no mistake and then she met that rich businessman from Athens and went off with him – good riddance I thought."

"Yes, I do remember . . . thought at the time it wouldn't last but wasn't there a child?"

"Yes, a girl and of course she went with her mother to Athens but Yannis would bring her home here for school holidays. I think her mother was pleased to get rid of her so she could spend more time with her lover. Anyway, it was the only time Yannis looked like his old self. She was a real child of the island and was never happier than when she was jumping off this jetty here with the other children; brown as a berry and swimming like a dolphin. Yannis would sit where you're sitting now sipping at a bottle of beer and telling anyone who passed about his beloved daughter. She's a young woman now . . . . how time flies . . . .she's off studying in London but she still comes here in the holidays to see her Dad.

Bring your sorrows and your heavy heart to our island in the sun
When you feel you can't go on with life here your healing has begun
We'll surround you with our friendship wallow in the Greek relaxing way
The atmosphere will tend your wounds just take it day by day

The flowers will lift your spirits the cats will make you smile
The sun will heat you to your bones your heart will thaw a while
Our beaches are so lovely the sea is warm and silky
Your skin will get a golden glow where once it was so milky

A week a fortnight all your life you're welcome here to stay
When once we came on holiday now we're here forever and a day
We welcome tourists to our country they brighten up our life
You'll feel relaxed and happy forgotten all the strife

Under My Umbrella

My fingers on the keyboard were sticky with sweat. The saying horses sweat, men perspire and ladies glow didn't apply at all as I was definitely sweating. It was running down my back, my hair was stuck to my scalp and my thighs were clinging to each other in a most unfeminine manner. *This is a waste of time today*, I thought as I turned off the computer.

It seemed longer than two years ago . . .

*****

"Ashes to ashes...."

The familiar words droned over me as I picked up a handful of soil, kissed the single red rose and dropped both onto the coffin lid. I felt empty. We had grieved together, Charles and I when we knew that he was dying. We faced his fears; I felt his pain and part of me died as he breathed his last.

But I remembered his words.

"You're still young, my darling. You must go on living.....why don't you go to our lovely island and write that novel...you know the one you've been threatening to write for years....and...don't be afraid to love again.....you've so much love to give...."

I heard the ewes call worriedly to their lambs in a nearby meadow, an early butterfly fluttered over the open grave landing momentarily on the heap of fresh brown earth and the scent of blossom floated on the mild air as nature burst into life after her long winter sleep.

Charles had loved spring. It was his favourite time of year. We had met in the spring and memories of our courtship crowded my mind. Walking hand in hand, ankle deep in bluebells in the woods, laughing together as we tried to avoid trampling the fragile flowers; passionate kissing under the heavy pink blossom of the cherry trees; swimming in the freezing sea, running out blue and shivering and trying to dress under the towels then giving up and falling naked into each other's arms. The memories shifted and focused in my head.

It was fitting that he should be returned to Mother Earth on such a day and I felt his liberation from suffering rise like a cloud from the grave; it seemed to engulf me, sending me a last message; I felt a hint of warmth in the spring sunshine and somewhere deep inside of my being I knew that I could start to rebuild my life.

Our two strapping sons stood by my side, towering over me protectively; one held my hand; the other had his arm protectively around my shoulder.

But I knew I would be fine. Oh yes, I would miss Charles dreadfully; my loving husband of almost thirty years. We had a good marriage. It had matured from crazy passion into a deep and special friendship but now it was over.

I straightened my shoulders from their hunch over the open grave, buttoned the jacket of my new black suit and turned, the two boys forever watchful, steeling myself for the many condolences that would flow my way from well-meaning friends and family.

But at last the final farewells had been made, the dishwasher loaded by willing friends and all there was to show for the afternoon were a few curling sandwiches sitting sadly on a lone plate.

"Are you sure you'll be OK on your own, Mum?" asked

Anthony.

I looked at the concerned faces of the boys.

"Yes…I need to be on my own…..I need to get used to it…but, of course I'll give you a call if I need anything."

They hugged me tightly as they left for their cars. I felt their concern and a lump rose in my throat. It had been hard for them as well; coping with the death of their father; taken from us all before his time.

The house echoed hollow and empty as I went from room to room touching furniture, fingering curtains, letting memories and tears flow; We had bought the house just after we married; it was an old rectory; empty and sad; needing lots of work and love to turn it into a home. It was really beyond our means but by dint of begging loans from family for the deposit and just managing to secure a mortgage based on our combined salaries, it was ours. It was on the edge of the village, a solid square stone building standing in a good sized garden. A garden that would be perfect for the family we planned. A house to grow old in…but that was not to be.

In the kitchen, I saw it as it had been way back then. An erratic solid fuel range dominated the space, an old sink, marked and chipped from years of use, with a wooden draining board. The boys had lain across the wood when they were toddlers while I had washed their gorgeous sweet smelling baby hair. We had a twin tub washing machine; a wedding gift from Charles' parents; it had come with a free blow heater. I remember being a bit put out when they kept the heater for themselves when we were desperate for some form of heating. Many hours of my life were spent hauling wet washing out of that tub with large wooden tongs and dumping it into the spin drier, which when turned on, caused the whole machine to waltz across the stone floor; white terry towelling nappies blowing on the line, soaking in buckets, baby bottles in bowls. Now it was state of the art units and appliances but it was still the heart of the house; the scrubbed pine table where the boys had pored over their homework, noisily playing and arguing over snakes and ladders, ludo and monopoly. My babies had grown, in a blink of an eye, from sitting strapped in high chairs to young men making their own way in the world.

Anthony was serious and responsible. He had a job in the city...I'd never really understood exactly what it was. He was married to Serena and they had a little girl called Lisa. Lisa was adorable. She was six years old and leggy, dark-haired and pretty with a button nose and hazel eyes. She reminded me so much of myself at that age. She loved books and when I visited we would spend time in a comfortable chair, her small body curled up on my lap while I read to her from my childhood favourites....Winnie the Pooh, Anne of Green Gables, What Katy did...oh how they all brought back memories of my own childhood. Unfortunately, as they lived in London, I only saw her a few times a year, so when I crystallised the plan lurking at the back of my mind I knew I could still keep up our very special relationship.

Bryan was charismatic and I knew he would always be able to charm his way through life. He worked for the media and was on short-term contracts but never seemed to be out of work and never seemed to be short of money. I knew that Charles had hoped that he would turn to a more secure way of making a living but it was what he had always wanted and it seemed that he was always in demand. He was not married but never seemed to be short of female companionship...a series of stunning looking girls had come and gone.....had been brought for a visit but usually only the once...then had never been seen again....that charm again!

As I let my fingers wander over the curtains in the lounge, I visualised the original ones. The fabric had come from the street market and peas could easily have been shot through it. I had proudly run them up on my mother's old treadle sewing machine. We were so pleased with the privacy that they afforded us. Now warm velvet curtains enhanced the room that was filled with furnishings chosen carefully and lovingly at auctions and second-hand shops; every piece had a memory attached; it was heart-breaking to look at it without Charles.

I traipsed slowly upstairs to the master bedroom. I saw Charles and me writhing in passion on the mattress on the floor; loving each other to pieces; conceiving our boys. Now it was a comfortable brass bed, thick pile carpet in which to wriggle bare toes and loads and loads of wardrobe space. It was a cool and soothing room; the colours were neutral except for the duvet set and that was deep autumn shades of terracotta and warm greens. The bed looked welcoming but I could visualise Charles lying there, wasting away, eaten from within by the unremitting cancer that had slowly but surely taken him from us.

But I knew without Charles' presence it was just a house; a building filled with inanimate objects. I would not allow it to become a mausoleum and I knew that in time I would turn my back on it. I hoped it would go to another young couple, setting out with the same hopes and aspirations that we had but that theirs would not be unexpectedly cut short as ours had been.

I squared my shoulders; it wouldn't be easy this step I was contemplating but Charles was expecting it of me.

*****

Charles and I had always been proud of our boys. I would dearly have loved a daughter but after Bryan some complications ensued that meant I would never have another child.

Anthony had been such a serious little boy. He always went off to school with his tie painstakingly tied, his blazer looking like new and his grey socks precisely pulled up to within a millimetre of each other. Bryan, on the other hand, had gone off with his school cap stuffed in his pocket, his tie askew and his satchel trailing on the ground; a real 'Just William'.

However neither of them had ever been a worry; a few of the normal boyish pranks; scrumping for apples, smoking behind the garden shed and trying out Charles' whisky which resulted in them both being violently sick. But compared to the terrible stories I had heard about other children I felt we had been incredibly lucky.

Strangely enough, it was Anthony who gave us our biggest shock when his girlfriend Serena became pregnant while they were both still at university. They immediately got married and although Serena gave up her studies when Lisa was born, Anthony kept going and now had his well-paid position in the city and we had gained a daughter in law and, of course, the adorable Lisa.

I had asked the boys to come to our house in Cheshire for the weekend. I thought it only fair that they should be apprised of the situation and be allowed their say in the matter.

"You're doing what….Mum are you sure…it's far too soon to make decisions…especially one like this…….anyway you can't sell the house…we grew up here... it holds all our childhood.....you're betraying Dad's memory......what about Lisa...she'll be devastated."

"Anthony.....I don't want to hurt ...but it's only a house...bricks and mortar...Dad didn't want me to stay drifting around here...keeping everything intact...until......until.... what? I know you think I'm past it...all children think that of their parents...but I'm only in my fifties...I could live for another thirty years...I need to do something for me.....now...please... please....try to understand. As for Lisa...I only see her a few times a year and I'm hoping that you and Serena will bring her to visit...and, of course, I'll make regular trips back. I promise I won't miss out on birthdays and all her special occasions."

Bryan, my youngest, always my baby, hugged me. I was constantly amazed at the size and strength of these boys that Charles and I had produced. They made me feel somehow small and fragile but that fragility masked an inner strength and I knew I would have to draw on all of that to see me through my plan.

"Mum, whatever you decide you know we'll always be here for you...it's just a bit of a shock.....but I suppose Greece isn't the end of the world...wouldn't you like to keep the house though...at least for a while....you could rent it out."

"No boys....it's....it's a fresh start...no clutching at yesterdays.....no looking back...Dad wouldn't have expected that of me."

*****

So I had sold up and moved to this Greek island; this small chunk of rock in the Aegean Sea where Charles and I had spent so many happy times.

It had been strange and a bit scary to disembark from the ferry without Charles organising the luggage and smoothing the way but friends we had made over the years were still here. I mentally gritted my teeth, brushed up on my limited knowledge of the language and found a new life slowly starting to emerge from the ashes of the old like the mythical phoenix.

I was lucky enough to find an apartment right on the harbour. It was small but so airy and cool with tiled floors and minimal furnishings. It was traditional Greek. I loved the faded turquoise colour on the wood that you only seem to find in Greece. I don't know if you can buy it faded or if it is the sun that does its usual work. There were cupboards in the most unexpected places; all sorts of nooks and crannies; the kitchen still had the old shallow traditional stone sink but there had been modern plumbing installed so the old sink now sported a large tub of geraniums tumbling their scarlet beauty into the room. Over the edge of my balcony purple bougainvillaea and peach hibiscus rioted happily and in profusion; this country that I had loved for many years always seemed to me to be a blinding mix of white or pastel coloured walls and garishly bright flowers; the sun forever bouncing and reflecting wherever you looked.

Sitting out on the balcony was better than any television programme and I missed nothing of the constant activity. I spent many happy hours watching neophyte sailors try to moor their hired boats; I smiled at the chaos that ensued when anchors became entangled deep under the water; I saw with amusement the amazing attire of the many visitors as they arrived on the ferries; and I heard the trundling of suitcase wheels on cobbles as people left at the end of their holidays and was always pleased that it wasn't me. Unfortunately it was too easy for me to become distracted from the writing that I had promised Charles I would do.

Anthony had spent two weeks here with the family and, as I had fully expected, Lisa had fallen in love with Greece. She spent most of her time swimming like a fish in the warm silky Aegean sea......I showed her the delights of the island....we ate at all my favourite tavernas and she went home brown as a berry and oozing good health.

Bryan had been out with his latest lady and, perhaps it was only wishful thinking, but I sensed a difference in this relationship. Bryan seemed to be as enthralled by Kathleen as she was with him...perhaps...perhaps...but only time would tell.

*****

I sighed as I closed the lid of my laptop. This novel wasn't going as well as I had hoped.....I slumped back in the chair, looked out over the harbour and felt the wetness trickle down my back. *A swim's in order*, I thought.

I changed into a swimsuit, slipped on shorts and a top, grabbed a towel and started around the harbour.

There must be a storm brewing, I thought. The air was oppressive and seemed to press down on me. I brushed away a lazy hornet hovering in the heavy air; a small lizard hung motionless on a wall; only his eyes darting on the lookout for mosquitoes. Feral kittens scattered from their play as my feet approached. I must look like a giant to them, I thought or perhaps they don't see things as we do.

As I passed the scooter hire kiosk I heard "*yiasou* Maria..." the friendly Greek greeting float out from under the awning. I looked around but all I could see in the dim interior was Yannis' strong brown forearms doing something technical to a bike. I firmly closed down any thoughts of these arms being anywhere near me; don't be silly at your age.

*****

I was sitting in the churchyard in the welcome shade of the tall dark Cypress trees. The cicadas were chirruping loudly as if attempting to drown out the chanting emanating from the open door of the church. I'm not at all a believer but the soft voice of the chanter and the sweet scent of the incense were quietly soporific and I felt calm and relaxed.

I love the cicadas. They start with a lone voice and gradually others join in until it is a swelling crescendo drowning out all other sounds. Then suddenly, as if some unseen conductor has dropped his baton, it stops and the ensuing silence is palpable until one rogue hidden deep within the foliage tentatively chirrups, others join and the whole cacophony starts again. To me, this sound is the epitome of long hot Mediterranean summers.

I had wandered into the churchyard as I could see that there was a service taking place possibly a name day and I sat at the back and watched the ladies, dressed almost predominately in black, as they went up to the front, dropped a coin in a box, lit a candle and crossed themselves. I've always found other cultures and religions fascinating.

I was aware of someone approaching and looked up to see a man; not any man but the most quintessentially Greek man. His wiry curly hair framed his dark olive skinned face but it was his eyes that had my complete attention. They were almost black; bottomless pools framed by jet black lashes. I felt something deep inside stir; something I thought was dead and gone.

"What is a beautiful lady doing sitting on her own?"

"I... well . . . my Greek isn't very good so I thought it best to sit here at the back."

"May I sit here too? . . . My name is Yannis."

He proffered his hand and I shook it trying not to notice the quiver of electricity that passed between us.

"Maria," I replied.

His English was impeccable and I silently vowed to try harder with my Greek.

We chatted quietly and the time flew.

I saw the Papa emerge and bless the bread and I gratefully accepted a slice with some cold water to wash it down.

The scraping of plastic chairs heralded the close of the service and people started to drift away forming and reforming in small groups to chat and catch up with neighbours and friends.

"I have enjoyed your company," Yannis said formally; then added, "Would you like to come for a drink with me sometime?"

I nodded . . . "Yes . . . that would be lovely."

And so it became a common occurrence for me to walk down to the hire shop when Yannis was closing up for the night and we would walk the back streets where only the most intrepid of tourists ever ventured. We would end up in the bar belonging to Stavros. A bar definitely for locals where old men played and argued over games of backgammon and feral cats dozed in safe corners oblivious to the odd cockroach scuttling across the stone floor.

Sometimes we went to the hotel and sat in the bar

with the tourists. Manolis, the owner and grapevine of the island gossip, would come and join us for a chat and ply us with complimentary ouzos.

Yannis was well known in these places and by association I was accepted.

He asked about my life and I told him about Charles and the boys.

"My wife left me for a rich man in Athens . . . she never really liked the

island... .and she preferred the money to me."

"Have you any children Yanni?"

"I have a beautiful and clever daughter. She is at university in your country . . . in London. She comes here whenever she can. She has the island in her soul . . . like me . . . she is her father's daughter."

The spark between us was scary and I knew that he felt it too. He would gaze at me with those hypnotic eyes and I felt I could drown in their depths. But we never even touched hands. It was as if we were both wary of stepping over an invisible threshold into a different place.

*****

The bike rental business was hard work and long hours in the summer keeping the tourists supplied with transport. It was easy to spot the tourists as they sat demurely on the bikes wearing their helmets. The locals, on the other hand, blatantly ignored the law and on a scooter you could see the whole family, the dog in the foot-well and Grandma sitting side saddle on the back. I never ceased to be amazed at how many people could squeeze onto a bike.

The stalls along the harbour were overflowing with

souvenirs waiting to be exchanged for the euros of the day trippers who regularly arrived for their holiday excursion.

'Day trip to an unspoiled island included in the price of your package!' I had seen the advertisements.

Yachts jostled cheek by jowl; the happy would-be sailors swabbing decks, coiling ropes and attending to the many chores that came with the hired boats.

Not my kind of holiday, I mused; much too much like hard work...now, if I was sailing....I'd have one of these huge gin palaces with all mod cons, flush toilets, proper showers and hot and cold running crew to attend to my every whim. I could see myself reclining on the deck on thick floral cushions nursing a pink gin...

Well, actually...I admitted to myself . . . I would settle for being swept off on the back of one of Yannis' scooters. I blushed at the thoughts starting to creep into my mind. I could almost hear Charles laughing......'go for it, girl'. Don't be silly Charles.

I came down to earth as a large fat raindrop hit my hand. Another one splattered at my feet leaving a damp mark as large as an old penny on the hot dusty ground. Thunder rumbled threateningly in the distance.

Perhaps no swim, I thought as I turned back. Abruptly the heavens opened in earnest. When it rains in Greece it doesn't hold back. Stair-rods definitely come to mind...the rain hammered down blotting out everything...the water in the harbour churned, turned grey and merged with the sky. In an instant I was saturated. My clothing clung like a second skin.

As I turned for home I noticed that everyone had miraculously disappeared; the people from the boats had scurried below decks and the stall holders had retreated as far back as they could into their cave-like interiors. I was totally alone in this world of streaming water.

As I squelched along in my flip flops the thick curtain of rain parted and Yannis appeared; with a flourish he opened a large black umbrella and raised it over my head. He smiled down at me with his blazing Greek smile and my heart turned a somersault. For the first time ever his arm went around my shoulders and he pulled me close. We seemed cut off from the rest of the world; safe inside our tiny shelter. His head bent towards me and his lips grazed mine.

Inside my head I heard Charles voice singing a line from the Hollies song from the sixties (was I really that old!).

"Love grows, under my umbrella."

*****

"I'm pleased for Yannis. He's a good man and deserves a good woman. Now my friend how about the festival this year? Was it up to its usual standard? I seem to remember it was a bit of a showpiece among the islands and people came from far and wide to participate. I used to love it as a boy when we sat on the wall by the bridge, watching and listening to what was happening on the stage and simultaneously eyeing up the girls . . . oh, those were the days."

"These were the days indeed . . . when money wasn't a problem but things have changed . . . . it's not as flamboyant as it used to be . . . as with everything else . . . times are tough and belts have to be tightened . . . but we still put on a good show using mostly local talent. The dancers as always danced their hearts out and how they do it in the heat and in these costumes I'll never know but they didn't let us down. Then there was the usual octopus festival . . ."

"No . . . I don't believe it . . . they still do the octopus . . . octopus and free retsina?"

"Exactly and it's always well attended . . . not just for the free food and drink but it's an integral part of the island culture."

"Do you remember when were boys . . . . we'd try and steal some retsina even although we weren't allowed . . . how we'd pose in front of the girls . . . we thought we were so macho . . . "

"I remember it well... .seems like yesterday . . . . Did I tell you about the girl who worked here last summer and met Michalis . . . no... .well she and Michalis had a good thing going and he wanted to marry her, they would sometimes come in for a late drink when she had finished work. A pretty little thing and she loved the island and dare I say it she loved Michalis but her family and friends were horrified at the idea of her marrying into a different culture, told her she would regret it etc etc etc so off she went back to the good old UK. Michalis was inconsolable. He came in here and got drunk out of his skull most nights then suddenly he disappeared. . . .poof!. . Left the island I heard. Well... lo and behold didn't little Anna book a holiday this year . . . you know I don't like to meddle but I did drop a word in Michalis' mother's ear as I guessed she would know where he had gone....."

Follow your heart life is too short to listen to them who tell you no

You'll make mistakes but better that than wondering if you'll ever know

The joy of love no matter not approved by well-meaning family and friends

It is your life and you don't want any regrets when it inevitably ends

Decisions sometimes not so wise but you won't get a second chance

Before you know it age will come make sure you've joined the happy dance

The merry go round the ups and downs the highs and lows are all the part

Of life that makes your world go round go now and follow your heart

Follow Your Heart

How could she have allowed herself to be persuaded to leave? Now it looked as if she was too late.

Loud music, loud voices, loud cicadas; the atmosphere was heady and Anna was happy to be back in Greece.

She watched the traditional dancing; the girls and young men in their colourful outfits whirling and bobbing to the twanging of the bouzouki. The smoke from the barbeque struggled sluggishly through the hot evening air, local ladies carried trays offering slices of octopus; the free retsina spurred the conversations to greater and noisier heights.

She never tired of watching the island people on these occasions. Plastic chairs were shifted around as more and more members of families arrived. The scratching of the plastic on stone slabs a constant sound as circles of people were formed then reformed. At the centre of each family group sat Grandmamma; the most important figure; the matriarch who was revered for her wisdom and experience of life. The family unit was inviolate. It was the glue that held together the fabric of the island.

And the children; babies in arms were passed from doting aunt to grandmother to cousins; toddlers unsteady on their baby legs explored their world safe in the enveloping love of their extended family; older children ran and laughed, they mimicked the dancers, climbed fences and learned about life and socialising without being aware; teenagers lounged; the boys in a group leaned nonchalantly, posing and pretending to ignore the girls who were in another group giggling and posturing in outfits as daring as their parents would allow; boys and girls whatever the culture or country unknowingly playing out the age old game. The game that makes the world go round.

Anna was reminded of a show that she had attended in the local hall in her village a few weeks before. It was her young cousin's dancing display and several members of her family had gone to support the budding ballerina.

Everyone sat quietly in rows and only murmured voices could be heard. Occasionally the sharp tones of a mother or father were heard telling a child to sit still or be quiet. There were no toddlers or babies. It seemed that they had all been left with babysitters. There were no large family gatherings or loudly raised voices. There were no grannies presiding as the matriarch of the family. There was no enthusiastic and uplifting atmosphere.

The one similarity was a group of teenagers at the back of the hall. As in Greece, they were sharply divided into boys and girls. The boys shrugged their leather jackets and apart from covert glances kept their eyes averted from the girls. The girls were openly giggling and eyeing up the talent. Their short skirts and skimpy tops seemed too exposed on a cold and rainy evening. But the game was the same.

Anna knew which culture she preferred.

She relaxed in her seat near the back of the square and inhaled the smoky barbeque aroma, the garlic being spread liberally on the cooking fish and a waft of the floral scent from the flowering bush behind her; evocative smells of Greece.

Anna had worked in Greece the previous summer. Long hours spent serving in a taverna had not left her much time for play but each morning before her shift began she would explore. Unlike the quintessential picture of Greece with blindingly white buildings, this island had a tumble of pastel coloured houses on two sides of the hill sweeping down to the harbour. At the back, the ground flattened out and there sat a magnificent church, a clutch of cafes and tavernas and the town square where the various events were staged during the annual festival

She would arrive at the beach before the tourists and swim in the crystal clear Aegean Sea.

She would revel in the feel of the water on her skin and afterwards, would stretch out for an hour on the rocks. The sun would caress her skin and all she could hear were the sound of the bells calling the congregations to the services, the soporific voices of the chanters emanating from the churches and an occasional donkey braying mournfully in the distance. She felt completely isolated in some kind of paradise.

By the time she was packing up and leaving to get ready for work the first few holiday-makers were setting up camp on the sun-beds. They unpacked books, i-pods and towels from capacious beach bags then started the arduous task of oiling up. Arms and legs were given a liberal application of factor whatever then husbands attended to their wives' backs and vice versa. They were preparing for a busy day broiling in the hot sun.

Michalis had been a regular at the taverna and they had started chatting. She began to look forward to his visits and was delighted one evening when he asked if she would join him for a drink afterwards.

There were only a few bars open by the time she finished up but they wandered comfortably through the quiet winding streets of the island's main settlement. A few places still served and some tardy tourists stubbornly sat nursing their metaxas, retsinas or ouzos not wanting to spend too much of their precious holidays sleeping.

Murmured greetings were directed at Michalis as chairs were stacked, tables wiped down and floors swept clean of the detritus of the evening ready for the next day's onslaught of thirsty tourists.

Although there were a limited number of tourists who could stay on the island every day several boats arrived in the harbour delivering hordes of day trippers to fill the tavernas at lunchtime, crowd into the cafes and bars in the afternoon and swell the coffers of the many stallholders selling typical tourist souvenirs.

In a narrow back street Michalis led her into a small bar tucked away from the usual tourist haunts.

"*Yiasou* Stavro," he called to the barman.

Only a few Greek men sat around. Some sat quietly nursing their drinks and a couple of them played a desultory game of backgammon. The only sounds were the click of the counters on the board and the soft ticking of worry beads. No background music to spoil the atmosphere. They all greeted Michalis and looked curiously at Anna. She was introduced to them as Michalis' friend and that was enough for her to be immediately accepted.

They had talked and talked. Anna's Greek left much to be desired but Michalis' English more than made up for it and, not for the first time, Anna was humbled by the inability of so many British to communicate with foreigners in their own tongue.

It became a regular thing for Michalis to wait until Anna had finished work and they would walk to Stavros' bar and chat for hours.

One evening a young man came in selling trinkets. He wheeled his wares around the bar and the customers tried out torches, battery operated fans and perused the selection of DVDs.

"I'll buy something for you," Michalis said and picked out a silver plated ring. The pattern was the Greek keys.

"These have many meanings," he said but didn't expand on his comment.

The ring was actually a man's ring and they laughed as she slipped it on finger after finger but finally the only one it fitted was her thumb. So she wore it there proudly.

Occasionally they went to the hotel for a late drink and they would sit at the edge of the water and chat to Manolis. It was a beautiful setting. The tables sat right at the side of the jetty and at their feet the water gave off a cool refreshing air.

One thing led to another and one night as he walked her back to her apartment, Michalis stopped, turned her towards him, lent down and kissed her gently.

"I think I love you," he whispered into her hair. "I've been trying not to...but....". He bent and kissed her again and she thought she was in heaven.

She would lie in bed each night smiling to herself and hugging dreams of Michalis.

Too soon the raging heat of the summer turned to the softer warmth of September and finally to October. The last charter flight came and went taking with it the last of the tourists.

It was the end of the season and she was due to go home.

"Don't go," he whispered insistently his lips moving against her neck. "Stay with me, my little love....I want to marry you.....I want to be with you forever...I want us to have many babies."

*****

"You're doing what!" her father had bellowed down the 'phone.

"Don't be stupid, Anna.....you know what'll happen......he'll dump you...sure as day.....you're nothing but a holiday romance," her sister was sharp and impatient at what she saw as Anna's stupidity.

"Different cultures, Anna....it'll never work......you're not Shirley Valentine you know.....don't be such a romantic," her friend sighed in irritation.

So she had left the land of blue skies and sunshine and returned to grey and rainy Britain.

She settled back in with her parents; into her

childhood bedroom; into her family routine and it was if the summer had never been. It was a lovely dream that didn't impinge on her life back in Britain.

A vacancy arose in a local office so she applied for it; was successful and tried to get back into her old life.

It wasn't all bad. Her friends of many years were fun and weekend nights out ended in giggles and taxis home before the inevitable hangovers on Sunday mornings.

However, she couldn't throw herself wholeheartedly into her friends' obsession with the boys. She knew that in previous years she would have been first up there talking about the sexiness or otherwise of the young men but now they all paled into insignificance when the image of Michalis popped into her mind.

"I like your ring," a friend's brother had said one evening. "I worked in Greece a few years ago and I understood that the keys are symbols of love and faithfulness . . . . although I could be wrong . . . . but I'm sure that's what was said."

At night she would toss and turn in bed her heart aching for Michalis. Her fingers played constantly with the ring on her thumb which she never ever took off. Did he really mean it as a sign of his love or was it wishful thinking? She could remember every detail; the touch of his hand; the feel of his lips on hers; hear his soft endearments being whispered in her ear. She couldn't but ponder on ...what if.....what if she had stayed. What was Michalis doing now? Was he missing her or had he found another willing tourist as all her friends had warned that he would?

She had to go back.

*****

So here she was in the blazing heat of August but

only for a two week holiday; better than nothing.

Of Michalis there was no sign.

No one had any knowledge of his whereabouts. Her disappointment was huge but for tonight she relaxed into the festival atmosphere and chatted in her limited Greek to the many friends who were pleased to see her back.

She looked around and noted that Yannis from the bike hire was still with his English lady and Manolis from the hotel was holding court among his many friends and family. He waved cheerily to her from across the square.

When she had been originally to the island she had rented a small studio but this time as it was only for a couple of weeks she had opted to stay in the hotel.

There was only one hotel on the island and it was owned and run by Manolis and various members of his family. When having drinks in the bar she had discovered that there was nothing on the island that Manolis didn't know about.

"I expect you've come back to see Michalis," he said to her surprise one evening.

"Oh yes, *koukla mou*, I know what was between you. There are no secrets from me. But Michalis left not long after you did and even I don't know where he is. He was distraught and inconsolable."

"Oh, Manoli . . . .I was so wrong to go back....I was so weak listening to my family and friends and now . . . .I'm too late," she stifled a sob.

*****

Then she saw him.

He was standing in the shadows at the edge of the

crowd. A brooding presence; almost invisible under a spreading dark tree; even the children gave him a wide berth. A young man walked over and clapped him on the shoulder in a friendly gesture but he shrugged it off moodily so the man retreated muttering to his group of friends.

He didn't look like her Michalis. His olive skin seemed darker, his black eyebrows beetled low over his eyes and instead of the relaxed stance she remembered his arms were folded across his chest and his whole demeanour screamed *leave me alone.*

Anna got up and slowly walked across the square. She skirted the dancers and carefully avoided low-flying children.

"*Yiasou* Michali," she said softly stopping a few feet in front of him.

He looked up and for a moment she saw a ray of hope burn in his eyes then the shuttered look returned.

"You came back...but you'll go again...back to nice safe Britain...back to your disapproving friends and family...back to the people who think I'm not good enough for the likes of you."

"Not this time," she whispered. "I was so wrong...but didn't realise it till I was back...I'm so sorry...I didn't mean to hurt....I've missed you so..."

"No second chance Anna......I...I can't..." his voice broke and she saw how hard it was for him to hold his emotions in check.

A lump filled her throat.

"Michali...oh, Michali...I'm..." she choked before a tear escaped and ran down her cheek; she lifted her hand to surreptitiously wipe it away.

As her eyes clouded with pain she felt his hand brush away her tear; she turned her head and kissed his palm.

"You're wearing my ring," he whispered.

"I've never taken it off . . . .it reminded me of you."

His other hand came up and he cupped her face.

"Don't hurt me again....my love...my love...I wanted to die...I couldn't bear.....please don't leave...."

"I won't...I promise...I'll cancel my flight...I'll stay...I can't leave....."

She melted into his arms and dampened his t-shirt with her tears.

They stood alone in the shadows clutching at each other while the music, the children and the loud voices washed around the edges of her consciousness.

*****

"So . . . I'm pleased that that worked out well; with a little help from you."

"Well, sometimes I feel a little help needs to be given . . . you know what I mean? Now . . . *filo mou...* .tell me are you staying this time or will you be off on your travels again soon?"

"No Manoli, this time I'm back for good. I've had my days of travelling. I want to spend whatever's left of my life here on the island. It's changed so much since the day I first left. Do you remember when there were no cars? It only seems like yesterday. The day the first car drove off the ferry we were all there . . . you and I couldn't take our eyes off it . . . . we wanted to touch it to sit in it to see it go. Now there are cars all over and not the roads to cope. But then it's a living working island; not a museum; people can't be denied the accoutrements of modern life just because we'd like to turn the clock back."

That's true my friend . . . very true . . . . every young person now seems to have a mobile phone glued to his or her ear but I dare say if we were their age we would be the same."

"Anyway . . . I hear old Manos has snared himself a pretty English rose. Is that true?"

"I actually think for the first time ever he is in love . . . can you imagine him thinking of anyone else but himself . . . but he worships the ground she walks on . . . . and between you and me if my instincts are as sharp as they used to be . . . I think there may be a baby on the way."

Sing your heart out as you were born to do
It's why you came to our enchanted isle
Don't listen to what people say to you
We want you to stay here for a while

You must enjoy our sea and sun and friendship
We welcome visitors with open arms
We think in Greece our island is the flagship
And we need the likes of you with all your charms

The Festival

He watched her bow to the audience and graciously accept a bouquet of flowers. Her soft blue dress complemented her English rose colouring and showed her slim figure to perfection. A hint of cleavage quickened his senses.

"Don't let it all go to your head. They're only a bunch of locals and tourists sitting in cheap plastic chairs. It's not exactly the Albert Hall," he hissed as she crossed behind the piano.

"Rehearsal here tomorrow morning at ten; you've still a lot to do."

With that, he turned on his heel and left. He tried to blot out the image of her grey eyes looking hurt and her soft mouth trembling slightly.

"Why is he always so nasty to me," she said to the sound engineer who was busily dismantling his equipment.

"I was so excited at the thought of singing in the festival and especially on this gorgeous Greek island and he's spoiling it all."

"It's just his way. Don't let it bother you. . . . . I know..... why don't I buy you an ouzo when I'm finished here? That'll cheer you up."

Sophie looked doubtful.

"I don't even know your name," she said.

"Vasilis..... now you know and you're Sophie. So we're introduced. Come on now."

She waited while he packed away the equipment – a place for everything and everything in its place. He was a real neat freak but she had to admit he was easy on the eye; typically Greek with olive skin, very dark hair and wonderful smile. However, he didn't do anything for her. There was no sexual spark.

Sophie walked with him to the harbour front and they sat in a small taverna sipping their ouzo. The holiday yachts were moored for the night and the only sounds were the slapping of rigging on masts, the creak of restless boats gently moving on the water and quiet chatting from the holiday sailors sitting on deck having a late drink.

The harbour looked stunningly beautiful. The lights from the houses twinkled on the hillside and reflected in the water and at first glance it didn't seem real but like some giant film set.

Vasilis was charming and easy to talk to and Sophie started to unwind.

"I couldn't believe my luck when I won the competition to come to Greece and sing in the festival and when I arrived it all seemed too good to be true. The island's even more beautiful than I had imagined. The sea is so clear and the swimming is unbelievable . . . and I can't believe there are still donkey trains working!"

"Oh yes. . . . .there's places up in the village where the roads are so narrow that the donkeys are the only means of delivering building materials etc. Did you know before the road was built the only way up to the village was through narrow lanes and up winding stone steps? It's said that the people of this island had the longest lifespan of any in Greece. Their hearts were so strong with going up and down from the harbour to the village coupled with our healthy diet. But now we have a road and everyone has cars and fast food has come even to here. So the kids sit in front of the television eating junk and getting fat. It's all very sad."

"I suppose you can't stop progress but it is a shame."

"Never mind about all that . . . . tell me where you live."

"I live in the south of England in a village. It's very pretty. The only downside is the weather. When I come to a place like this I realise how much I love the sun and the heat."

"So you entered this singing competition?"

"Yes . . . . .I won the local heat, then the area one and went to London for the final and here I am. I've never been abroad before so coming here on my own was an enormous step but Manolis in the hotel is keeping a fatherly eye on me."

"You're quite safe here on the island. There's very little crime. It's difficult to commit a crime on a small island as you can't escape unless there's a ferry about to leave and even then there would probably be police waiting for you at the other end."

"Anyway I thought I'd reached heaven then Manos came into my life and he's gone out of his way to make my time here hell. What have I ever done to him?" Her eyes were bright with unshed tears and her lip trembled.

"Well.....I think you're great," Vasilis said encouragingly and smiled his charming Greek smile.

He walked her home through the small winding streets. Shop doors were still open giving tantalising glimpses of their Aladdin's cave interiors. The tavernas were slowing down for the night but a few tourists, reluctant to give over any of their holiday time to sleep, were nursing their drinks and chatting softly. Some locals were sitting on their balconies and the quiet click, click, click of worry beads followed their progress.

At the hotel entrance, Vasilis turned her towards him obviously looking for at least a kiss but Sophie turned her head and his lips landed on her cheek.

"Goodnight, Vasili. Thank you for the drink. I enjoyed your company. See you tomorrow at rehearsal," she said as she slipped through the door.

"You watch that young man," said Manolis as she passed through reception. "He's a charmer but he's after every pretty girl who comes here."

"Thanks Manoli . . . I'll be careful. *Kalinichta*."

The first heat of the competition had been held in the village hall.

Sophie thought she would have a good chance as she was a regular in the drama group and a member of the church choir.

When she got up on the stage and faced family and friends she knew she looked good and she sang with confidence.

The judges were unanimous in their choice of Sophie as the winner.

It was a wonderful evening. The ladies of the village had supplied sandwiches and homemade cakes and there was plenty of lemonade and tea to quench the singers' throats.

The area heat was more formal and was to be held in the market town hall.

Sophie was much more tense this time. This was not her village friends and neighbours. These were judges who had never heard of her and the other competitors were winners from their small towns and villages.

Backstage they all gathered nervously. Some were quietly warming up their voices, others clutching their song sheets and muttering to themselves and others like Sophie were trying to find a quiet corner to try to relax and keep calm.

Sophie was eleventh out of twenty and before she realised it she was being ushered on to the stage. She centred herself and as she heard her introduction took a big breath into her diaphragm and gave it all she could.

In the opinion of the judges she was the clear winner and would go through to the final in London.

"Oh....Mum... I'm so nervous. What'll I wear . . ."

"Come on now . . . . you'll be wonderful. Dad and I will be there cheering you on. I know... .let's go shopping and find a nice dress."

Sophie had a lovely girlie day with her Mum in the shopping mall.

They went in and out of shops trying on various outfits. They giggled at the outrageous ones and sighed longingly over the expensive ones.

Just when they were giving up hope of ever finding something suitable they spied a small shop that they had missed the first time around.

Sophie saw a crossover dress and hung it in the changing room. Then she followed it with a snazzy little black number. Mum handed her a pale blue dress but privately Sophie thought it hung like a rag but she was willing to try anything.

Her Mum fell about laughing when she emerged with the crossover.

"You look like the cleaning lady we used to have when

I was a child... oh no I don't think so!"

As Sophie emerged again Mum had another fit of the giggles.

“The judges will think you’re trying to seduce them . . . have you looked in the mirror?”

"Yes....I did think it was a bit vampish."

"A bit... .your dad would die of embarrassment. Go and try the other one."

“I don’t really fancy it but ok.”

When Sophie looked in the mirror she couldn’t believe what she saw. The dress’s soft fabric that looked like a rag on the hanger moulded itself to her body. It wasn’t at all cheap looking just beautifully feminine.

As she walked out of the fitting room her Mum gasped and her eyes filled with tears.

“I can’t believe I have such a beautiful woman for a daughter,” she choked.

So the choice was made and the purchase completed.

Sophie and her Mum treated themselves to lunch and a glass of wine to celebrate.

"We should do this more often, Mum... .it's been a lovely day."

On the day of the competition, she travelled with her parents by train. They were staying in a hotel close to the competition venue.

. She dressed carefully in her lovely blue dress and applied her makeup with special care.

As she waited in the wings her legs were shaking so much she thought she wouldn’t be able to walk out on stage. The other competitors seemed so good she was tempted to go home.

All too soon it was her turn and she willed herself to walk out into the spotlight.

For a terrifying moment she couldn't remember what she was going to sing; couldn't think of the opening line; couldn't bring to mind the first note.

However, once she started to sing she forgot everything else. Her world narrowed down to the microphone and the sound of her own voice.

She sat with her parents while the results were read out.

"The quality of the singing was extremely high and the judges had a difficult time tonight. However, I have in these envelopes the names of the first three and I'll read them in reverse order."

Sophie gripped her Mum's hand.

Oh if I could only come in the top three I will be happy, she thought.

"Third is Natalie Brown."

Natalie walked on to the stage smiling broadly and received her certificate.

"Second is Anne Macintyre."

Anne stood up to the applause and collected her certificate.

That's it, thought Sophie; *I was so hoping to be in the top three.*

She was wallowing in her disappointment so much that she didn't hear the announcement of the winner.

"It's you Sophie... .you've won."

She looked at her Mum who was attempting to push her to her feet.

She walked up to the on to the stage in a daze completely unable to believe it.

The judge shook her hand and presented her with her winning certificate to tumultuous applause.

"And the winner also receives this fabulous opportunity to travel to Greece all expenses paid and sing in the festival."

*****

Next morning promptly at ten Sophie appeared in the churchyard where the concerts were being staged. Intricate pebbled mosaics covered the ground, the church building stood stolidly as it had done for centuries and the tall dark cypress trees stretched up to the brilliant blue sky which was visible between the tops.

This is such a beautiful setting, she thought. *Everything is perfect except for Manos.*

Vasilis was fiddling with the speakers and winked encouragingly whenever she caught his eye.

Manos was waiting for her and they spent three hard hours rehearsing but no matter how hard Sophie tried in Manos' eyes she could do nothing right.

"No... .no . . .that note's not good enough... and again and again." He went on and on.

After a snack lunch, Sophie decided to go for a swim to relax. She was tense and overwrought after the long hours of trying unsuccessfully to please Manos.

She found a place on some flat rocks away from the tourists on the beach, spread her towel out and lay down.

The sun caressed her skin, the scent of the wild herbs soothed her senses and faintly in the distance she heard the dull clang of goats' bells.

Oh, this is heaven, she thought as she dozed a little.

Time for a swim; she lowered herself off a large rock and dropped into the crystal clear Aegean Sea. It was like silk caressing her skin and she swam out into the bay.

Almost back at the rocks she turned on her back and floated totally relaxed on the cool buoyant water.

Manos walked along the shore angry with himself for being so hard on Sophie. He knew within his heart that he found her attractive but he also knew she would never look at someone like him.

I must be twenty years older than her to start with, he thought. She's a foreigner; different ideas; different cultures etc. It would all be too difficult. How she would laugh if she could read my thoughts.

A lone swimmer caught his eye. As she turned on her back and floated he saw it was Sophie.

Pleased to be able to watch her unnoticed, he revelled in the sight of her slim body in the skimpy bikini, skin golden after her days in the sun and her fair hair fanned around her head like a halo. He longed to hold her. Not just hold her; he smiled ruefully as he felt his body respond.

He was aware of the speedboat passing but was lost in his thoughts. Suddenly he looked up in horror as the wave from the wake of the boat swept towards Sophie.

"Sophie, Sophie," he yelled in vain.

He scrambled down the rocks slipping and sliding but was helpless to stop the water lifting Sophie and throwing her against the rocks like a rag doll. She rolled back off the rock into the water face down.

He threw himself down on the rock unheeding of his

shins and elbows scraping on the rough surface, grabbed her by the arm before another wave could do any more damage and hauled her out of the water as the second smaller wave rushed onto the rock and soaked them both.

"Wake up please, Sophie. Are you ok? Sophie, oh Sophie please open your eyes."

Where am I, she thought as her eyes flickered. She looked up into Manos' face and quickly shut her eyes again.

I'm dreaming, she thought, *I'm dreaming that I'm in Manos' arms and he's not looking angry.*

"Wake up. How could you be so stupid to swim on your own? I don't believe you've done this."

She felt herself pulled to her feet and shaken.

I'm not dreaming, she thought. *It's him and he's hacked off at me again.*

"Why is everything I do wrong," she whimpered as her eyes opened again.

"Don't you know it's madness to do what you just did? You could have drowned if I hadn't walked by. How could you be so stupid?"

With that, he bent his head and kissed her hard on the lips and she felt the roughness of his skin grazing her face.

"And I've wanted to so that since I first met you but you've been besotted by that young Vasilis."

The kiss touched senses in Sophie that she didn't know existed. She looked up and touched his face in wonder.

"And I know it won't work," he barked. "I must be at

least twenty years older than you; you're a foreigner and only here for a short time. Why on earth am I doing this?"

Sophie shook her head. She was still slightly stunned and really couldn't understand all that was going on but she did know that she wanted Manos to kiss her again... .and again. So she leaned against his wet t-shirt and looked up at him.

"And don't look at me like that woman . . . don't you know what you're doing to me?"

"Can we sit down... .I'm a bit shaky."

He lowered her gently onto her towel and sat beside her but not touching.

"Firstly I'm not besotted by Vasilis. He took me for a drink as I was upset because you kept shouting at me. Secondly, thank you for saving me and I promise to be more careful in future and thirdly... .I'd really like you to kiss me again."

She wriggled along nearer to him and smiled. She had no fear of him now. She had seen inside the outer shell and knew there was a soft centre lurking unseen.

He put his arms around her and drew her gently to him. She knew all was going to be well.

*****

"Well . . . good for him . . . who would've thought it? He always was a curmudgeonly old sod. I must look for him and see the new pleasant Manos. I remember him well as a boy... .always in trouble . . . always ready to give some lip . . . but he did well when he went off to study music . . . where was it? Oh yes, London . . . . wondered how they could afford it myself although there was some rumour of a scholarship. . . . . So what else has happened this summer?"

"There was this lovely couple who seemed to have lost touch for years then met up again in Athens of all places seeing as they're British."

I thought you'd be with me forever
Our passion was real so I thought
The happiness to me that you brought
Touched me down in the depths of my soul
You were my rock you made me whole
But you had secrets that you could not share
When you left it was more than I could bear
I thought you'd be with me forever

Don’t Leave Me

Sheila loved the names of the stations on the Athens railway- Faliro, Moschato, Kalithea. They tripped off the tongue like poetry.

“How do you fancy a few days in Athens,” Paul had asked one evening.

“I have to go on business but I’ll have plenty free time. I thought that although my head office is in Piraeus we could stay somewhere central and explore the city.”

They had only been seeing each other for a few months but the relationship seemed to Sheila very intense on both sides. They hadn’t got to the stage of moving in together but she knew that it was only a matter of time.

They had met at a disco in town. Sheila had gone with a group of girls and they had giggled about meeting the love of their life the way that girls have always done since time immemorial.

Paul was leaning on the bar when it was Sheila’s turn to go for the drinks. There was an instant spark the way it happens in books but never in real life.

“How about you take the drinks back to your friends and come back and have yours here with me,”

As a chat up line it left a lot to be desired but Sheila was more than happy to do as he asked and she never did go back to her friends. It was ‘love at first sight’ and it continued unabated. It only took a few dates before they ended up in bed and it was all that Sheila had hoped for and more.

"I would love it . . . oh, Paul what a wonderful idea.

I'm due some holiday . . . . when are you, I mean we, going?"

"Next week. I got a call from the head office and they want to see me as soon as possible."

"What is it exactly that you do?"

"Nothing interesting . . . only a boring old office job."

It was a wonderful city and they had done all the tourist things. The open top bus had allowed them to get their bearings and decide what they wanted to further explore. And so they had wandered in the hot sun around the ruins of the Parthenon, browsed the expensive shops deciding what they would buy if they had unlimited funds and laughed as they struggled through the crowds in the Monastiraki flea market meanwhile holding tightly to wallet and handbag.

Paul's generous business expenses had meant that they could stay in luxury in a wonderful hotel in Syntagma Square and it all seemed to Sheila to be too good to be true and she would pinch herself as she lay in the huge bed snuggled into Paul. It was like being on honeymoon. After the sightseeing and Paul's business meetings they would hurry back to the hotel and fall into bed to enjoy wonderful passionate lovemaking. They made love on the bed, in the shower, on the floor and whenever and wherever they felt like it.

Sheila liked to go and wander around the busy old port of Piraeus while Paul was at his office and they had been on this rail line almost every day and thus she knew the stops off by heart and loved to admire the disparate stations as the train stopped and started.

The carriages were always packed and this day was no exception. Sheila had been offered a seat by a kind man and was squeezed into a corner by the window surrounded by Greeks on mobile phones, chatting in loud voices and trying to find spaces for large bags of shopping. The language was a complete mystery to her but she enjoyed the atmosphere. She couldn't see Paul but knew he was standing in the crowd near the doors. She rested her forehead on the window as the train stopped at Kalithea and smiled as people tried to crowd on to the train as the others tried to fight their way off.

Her head jerked up in surprise.

As the doors slammed shut the last person jumped clear and walked towards the exit. It was Paul. He passed her window without a backward glance.

She didn't know what to do. She struggled out of her seat and pushed her way to the door but, of course, they were locked shut as the train gathered speed. It was as if she were in the midst of a nightmare. At the next station Moschato she alighted and as the train left she stood alone on the platform realising she didn't have a clue what to do.

Paul never ever returned and when she looked back she didn't know how she had the strength to return to the hotel, pack everything including Paul's few things and fly home.

Her little flat in North London seemed cold and unwelcoming but she was glad that she and Paul had never moved in together as there were very few things to remind her of what they had or what she thought they had.

Time moved on as it always does and the pain and confusion faded into a nasty memory.

Mark was all that Paul wasn't. He was sensitive, loving and gentle and he was just what Sheila needed to salve her broken soul and restore her confidence.

They married after a long and low key courtship, in a quiet registry office service. They bought a cottage in Norfolk as Mark had accepted a transfer to Norwich and settled to married life.

It was never a passionate relationship and Mark's love-making was gentle and considerate and only ever in bed. Sometimes in the night she ached for Paul's passion and variety. She occasionally smiled to herself when she remembered all the different places that they had made love. Then she was dragged back to the present and the fact that Paul had walked away from her so she pushed it to the back of her mind and gave herself completely to her husband.

Sheila loved motherhood. Her two children were the centre of her universe. From the first time that her baby daughter was placed in her arms her whole being felt centred on this tiny scrap.

"Let's call her Grace after my mother," Mark suggested and after a long and difficult labour, Sheila was willing to agree to anything.

Two years later her son was born.

He was William after Sheila's father.

She revelled in her babies. When they were toddlers she would walk with them in the woods; one in the pushchair and the other hanging on grimly her little legs going like pistons to keep up. She imbued them with her love of nature as they stopped to admire the wildflowers and they all loved to catch sight of the wildlife. They would hold their breath in wonder as the deer flew across the paths silently and magically.

When they were at school she spent endless hours with homework and class projects. Their three heads would be bent over the kitchen table in concentration or up to their elbows in glue and cardboard.

But of course in no time at all they were young adults and ready to find their own feet... Grace went to university and landed a top job as a scientist and seemed set to be a career girl. William met and married a local girl; they settled in a cottage in the village and had already produced one daughter and Sheila had no doubt that there would be more.

Her relationship with Mark drifted into a comfortable, but if she was honest, rather boring rut.

"We never make love now," she said one evening after a few glasses of wine.

"We don't need all that stuff at our age . . . . don't be silly."

So she stifled her desires, told herself she was too old for all that and firmly dismissed any passionate thoughts that featured Paul.

Mark took to working late on a regular basis but it didn't bother Sheila at all as she liked her personal space.

One evening when they were having supper at the kitchen table Mark cleared his throat.

"I've... .er . . .something to tell you," he stuttered. "I've met someone else. I didn't mean it to happen . . . . but... .well . . . .I don't want to hurt you . . ."

"Come on Mark; spit it out; who is she?"

"It's not a she," he whispered going beetroot red.

Sheila was speechless but looking back she remembered his lack of interest in sex and after some thought, she wasn't really surprised.

I should have guessed, she thought, as I've known what a red-blooded male is really like.

It was an amicable divorce and Mark was generous in his settlement and so she was left financially comfortable.

She relished her single status, loved having the house to herself and never for one moment missed having Mark in her bed.

Although she loved her granddaughter dearly Sheila felt the need to do something for herself. She racked her brains for ideas. Then one night while lying quietly in bed enjoying the fact that she had the whole bed to herself she remembered Athens and how much she had loved the city.

I'll go there again. I'll visit all the lovely places.

She could hardly wait to get started. She spied a two-centre holiday in one of the Sunday supplements and decided that a week in Athens and a week on a Greek island sounded perfect. At last, it was all booked and she was on the flight.

It seemed no time at all until the captain gave the usual instructions about seat backs, tables and hand luggage and in minutes they were on the ground.

Athens airport was all new to her as it had recently been built for the Olympics but undaunted she collected her case and headed for the taxis.

The package holiday featured a week in Athens staying at the same hotel in Syntagma Square.

The hotel had been refurbished and for this she was grateful as there were no reminders of Paul.

She visited the old haunts. Her hotel window looked over Syntagma Square and she could watch the changing of the guard and wonder afresh at the strange gait of the marching soldiers.

She visited the wonderful new Acropolis Museum that had opened since her last visit. Walking in on the glass floor over the excavations gave her moments of disquiet but once inside the light flooding through the huge expanses of glass took her breath away and showed the marble artefacts to perfection.

On the last day she grabbed her courage and decided to take the train to Piraeus. She whispered the long-forgotten station names to herself and when she came to Kalithea she remembered the shock of seeing Paul walk away without a backward glance.

Her nose was pressed against the glass as the passengers went through the usual bun fight of people leaving the train fighting their way past the ones pushing their way on.

There was, of course, no magical reappearance of Paul.

She left the train at Piraeus and wandered out into the busy street. It was as she remembered it bustling, noisy and with the distinct salty smell of the sea. The big ships were lined up alongside the various quays loading and unloading their cargoes.

Tomorrow, she thought, I'll be on one of these on my way to the island.

She wandered aimlessly watching the hives of activity until she realised she was outside the head office of the firm that Paul had worked for.

She sat in a café opposite, ordered a coffee and watched the comings and goings.

Suddenly she froze in her chair. Paul was walking down the steps of the building. She half rose out of her seat then sat down again.

What to do?

Should she call him? Even after all these years and all he had put her through her heart still beat faster at the sight of him. He was older, of course. A little greyer around the temples, a little thicker around the waist but unmistakeably Paul.

He was coming straight for her and as he passed she whispered his name.

"Paul….."

He turned looking puzzled then a look of recognition spread across his face.

"It can't be... Sheila . . . is it really you?"

They stood looking at each other for what seemed like an eternity.

"May I join you?" He asked hesitantly.

"Of course," she gestured to the seat opposite.

"I don't know what to say . . . .what I did to you all these years ago . . . .it was unforgivable but I had no choice . . . I was under orders. You've no idea how it hurt . . . .how I missed you . . . .oh god how I missed you." He dropped his head into his hands.

"What do you mean following orders? What did you do? You told me you had a boring office job."

"I know . . . .it was all top secret. I didn't know when they summoned me to Athens that they had a job lined up and I had to go right away and tell nobody. I explained about you but they said I must leave you and disappear. They would brook no argument so there was no choice, At least I knew that the hotel was all paid for and you had your return flight so I knew you would be ok in that respect. So for years I lived undercover and when the job was completed, successfully, I may add . . . .it was too late. I thought you would have found someone else . . . . would never want to see me again after the way I abandoned you . . . .and so I didn't try to get in touch. And now here you are, I can't believe it."

"I don't know what to say, Paul. I was devastated when I saw you walk out of the station that day. I don't know how I managed to get back home all in one piece."

"I know . . . I know . . . .I've been torturing myself for years . . . .I don't suppose you can ever forgive me?"

"I don't . . . . ."

"Anyway tell me about yourself . . . what you're doing here for a start?"

"I'm on holiday; a week in Athens and a week on an island. This is my last day here and tomorrow I get on one of these huge ships over there and the day after I disembark at the island. Other than that I have a broken marriage behind me but I have been blessed with two children and a granddaughter. How about you?"

"I never married . . . .I had one or two relationships but nothing of any consequence . . . let's be honest there was nobody who could live up to you and what I thought we had together before I ruined it all."

Sheila declined to tell him how much she had longed for him all through the long years since they had been together.

"Would you consider having dinner with me tonight?"

Sheila hesitated but then thought *why the hell not.*

"Yes, that would be lovely."

"Where are you staying?"

"The same hotel in Syntagma Square."

"Really! OK, I'll meet you in the lobby about seven thirty if that's OK with you."

"That will be fine."

"OK must go . . . .see you later."

With that, he got up, leaned over and kissed her on the cheek and was gone.

She thought she heard him whisper.

"I'm so sorry."

The concierge called her to tell her she had a visitor in the lobby so she made her way down in the lift wondering if this was a good idea but as she saw him her heart skipped a beat and she knew whatever happened she would enjoy this evening.

They ate at a quiet restaurant not far from the hotel and as they were enjoying an after dinner metaxa Paul slid his hand across the table and covered hers.

The touch of his hand brought memories flooding back and although she knew she shouldn't she longed for him. Just one more time, she thought. So she turned her hand palm upwards and gently squeezed his.

They walked without speaking back to the hotel and up to her room.

"Are you sure?" he whispered.

No answer was required. She stepped into his arms and all the years in between melted away and it was as if they had never been.

"Would you mind if I came with you to the island?" he whispered as he held her afterwards, "I can't bear to lose you again."

"Oh . . . .please come. I'll change all the bookings to doubles. I can't believe I've found you and it's as if we've never been apart, Just don't leave me again."

"I promise I won't. Wild horses wouldn't drag me away from you now."

They shared a cabin on the ship and the following morning disembarked into the chaos of people, cars and lorries all trying to get on and off at the same time. The ferry being the lifeblood of the island there was always great excitement when it arrived.

They saw Manolis from the hotel holding up a card with Sheila's name and struggled through the crowd to reach him.

"The hotel's just around the corner ....let me take your case . . . .now follow me,"

Their room was perfect with a small balcony overlooking the sea. It faced east and they slept with the window open and the rising sun would wake them; its golden fingers creeping across the bed where they both lay naked.

They started each day by making love and then set off to explore. It was so beautiful. Every corner turned brought an even more spectacular view; the water was crystal clear, the scent of the wild herbs permeated the warm air and the only sounds were the clanging of the goat bells and the insistent chatter of the cicadas.

They swam in the sea and revelled in the feel of the silky water. They explored the interior of the island walking through the cool pine forests.

One evening they went to a concert in the churchyard. The featured singer was a pretty young English girl with the most amazing voice. The notes seemed to rise up through the warm velvet darkness between the dark forbidding cypress trees to the star-studded sky.

As they walked back hand in hand Sheila felt she couldn't be happier.

"Would you like to have a metaxa with me?" Manolis asked as they entered the foyer.

"That would be lovely . . . let's sit out by the water."

As they waited for their drinks Sheila realised that

Paul had gone quiet. She turned to him in time to see him clutch his chest.

The doctor was called, the helicopter summoned but it was all too late.

"You promised you would never leave me again," was all Sheila could sob over and over again.

Decisions had to be made whether to have the body taken back to the UK but Sheila decided on an island burial. She knew he had no family and they had been so happy in this paradise she thought he should rest here.

As he was lowered into the grave she promised she would always love him and would come back soon. She wouldn't leave him.

*****

"So there was a death . . . how sad. I always think it's strange how one person leaves this world and another arrives. They say God works in mysterious ways and who are we to question . . . . how about another drink my friend?"

Manlois went to the bar to refill our glasses. The breeze had died altogether and the sea at our feet was inky black and merged with the darkness of the sky so that it was impossible to see where one stopped and the other started. The stars twinkled in the heavens and I got this feeling that all's right with the world... .at least in the small part of the world that I knew.

Manolis came back with our glasses recharged and we sipped in silence absorbing the tranquillity of our little piece of heaven.

"Did you hear about Giorgos and Despina and all their troubles . . . . I totally blame Giorgos . . . .if he hadn't been so obsessed with that damn café she wouldn't have been lured into temptation... .but there you go we see all human life here on the island."

Don't abandon me, my love
I get so lonely and you never see
What your obsession is doing to me
You never look at me or take my hand
The business is your life and that is grand
But…don't abandon me, my love

Don't abandon me, my love
There's others out there who would take your place
Loneliness attracts a friendly face
I need a smile a touch for feeling good
To lift my spirits stand where you once stood
Please..don't abandon me, my love

The Affair

Dark, forbidding and unapproachable.

I can't believe this is the man I married, Despina thought. *I wish we'd never opened that damned café.*

When Despina had first met Giorgos he was running a small taverna with a very limited range of dishes. However, it didn't stop her from going there at every available opportunity. She went solely to watch the good looking and charming owner. This was not lost on Giorgos and when he had finished cooking and serving he would sit and chat with her.

"Would you like me to help with the clearing up?" she asked tentatively one evening.

"Oh no . . . . .I can't expect my customers to do that."

"But I'd really like to help." She said hoping it would buy her more time with him.

"OK but your meal's on the house."

And so it became a regular thing that Despina would stay until all meals were served and cleared away then she would go into the kitchen and tackle the washing up together with Giorgos.

They would bustle around together talking and laughing.

One night she turned from the sink holding a freshly washed glass dish just as Giorgos passed. They bumped into each other and the glass slipped from her wet hands and shattered on the stone floor.

"Oh I'm so sorry," she stuttered.

"No no it was my fault . . . . I'll get the brush . . . .just be careful of the glass."

Giorgos carefully swept up the shards of glass and dumped them in the rubbish.

Despina watched, lips trembling as she thought he'd never allow her back after being so careless.

"What's the matter," she heard him ask as she vainly tried to hold back her tears.

"You won't want me here again . . . . .and I enjoy it so much."

"Don't be silly. Accidents happen."

She felt his finger wipe the tear from her cheek and she opened her eyes to see his face only inches from her own. It seemed only natural for her to lean slightly forward and into his arms and she felt his lips gently touch hers.

"Oh I've wanted to do that for so long," he whispered into her hair. "You're so beautiful."

And so it continued that Despina helped clear up but afterwards they would wander off to a bar far from the tourist trail and chat for hours.

Despina loved the stroll through the narrow streets late at night when only a handful of people were still about. The warm velvet of the Greek night seemed to wrap itself around them and high above a million stars twinkled in a navy blue sky. The feral cats were up and about and dozens of them would eye them balefully from nooks and crannies, cockroaches would scuttle away from under their feet and sometimes a harmless snake would slither across their path.

The air was heavy with the scent of flowering bushes and petals of bougainvillaea and geraniums would cling to their shoulders as they brushed passed them in the narrow streets.

One evening as he was giving her a goodnight kiss outside her parents' house he whispered.

"I want to marry you...I can't bear to have to leave you every night...I want you to be mine completely."

"Oh, Giorgo... oh... yes please."

The wedding was all that a Greek wedding should be.

Despina walked to the bridge in the harbour with her entourage preceded by her uncle playing his accordion. Giorgos was waiting and as is tradition he carried the bouquet to present to her with a kiss as they met.

The church service was a blur of family and friends, the chanter's soft voice, the scent of the incense and the exchanging of the tied head-dresses.

Later at the hotel, Manolis didn't let them down with a spread fit for a bride and groom, lashings of local wine and a magnificent cake.

As is the custom Despina's family had provided them with an apartment fully furnished and ready to move into. When they arrived tired but happy after their big day Despina suddenly felt quite shy. It was not that she didn't want Giorgos in the biblical sense but wasn't sure what was expected of her.

They went into the bedroom; first she had to clear the bed of a mountain of sugared almonds left from the bed making evening. She swept them into a bowl and as she turned Giorgos was behind her. He took the bowl, laid it on a shelf then kissed her gently.

"It'll be all right *agapi mou*. I'll look after you."

He helped her step out of her wedding gown and as she slipped out of her underwear he quickly stripped off. The fan above the bed slowly rotated as his lips and fingers coaxed sensations from her body that had her gasping and when he slowly entered her there was only a slight twinge and at last she was completely his.

Despina loved to cook and now she had a free hand in the taverna. She prepared a variety of good Greek food which was served by Giorgos.

Tourists and locals alike enjoyed the tasty dishes, the happy atmosphere and the setting under a big shady tree.

Giorgos and Despina would arrive early to set up the tables and prepare the food ready to open at midday. After the last lunches had been served and cleared away, usually around three thirty they would go home for a siesta.

The shutters would be closed against the fierce afternoon sun and the ceiling fan would whiffle cool air over their naked bodies and Giorgos' hands and lips would transport her to delights she had never imagined existed. They would fall asleep sated with love before showering and readying for the evening influx of hungry customers.

Things couldn't be better.

"I've been thinking, *agapi mou*. As I see it there's an opening for a café on the square. Locals, tourists and day-trippers seem to congregate there and there's nowhere to sit and have a coffee or a drink,"

Worryingly the setup costs were much more than they had anticipated. However, the opening night was a triumph, way beyond their expectations. Despina joined the fun after the taverna closed and they returned home exhausted but happy.

In order to recoup their outlay, Giorgos became obsessed and spent from six in the morning until the last customer left, usually around midnight serving, cleaning and chatting.

Despina was left to run the taverna with the help of a young girl. Admittedly it really ran itself but siesta time wasn't the same without her husband. She would lie on the big bed watching the rotating fan and long for their afternoons of love. Her husband was a stranger now, working all hours that God gave him and retreating into an impenetrable shell.

"We can't go on like this. You're making yourself ill..........our marriage is suffering," she tried to reason with him but he refused to discuss it and shut himself away inside his brooding darkness.

The Englishman started appearing for lunch every day, sat at the same table, sometimes reading but most of the time just watching the world go by.

"What's your name?" he asked Despina one day in halting Greek.

"Despina, what's yours? Are you staying on the island? You seem to have been here for a while," she replied in perfect English.

"Why is it that you can all speak English and we can only stutter a few words of Greek?" He asked.

"Well, we all have to learn English at school. You see there's nowhere outside of Greece that the language is spoken so to communicate with the rest of the world we have to be fairly fluent. In any case, dealing with tourists is essential that I can understand them."

"Anyway my name's Roger; I'm here for a few months. .....I'm trying to write a novel," he smiled ruefully. "But struggling a bit....actually.... struggling quite a lot."

Despina found herself looking forward to his chats. He always seemed to be there when she had finished cooking and tidying up ready to shut for the afternoon.

"You're married to the man in the café on the square," Roger said one day.

"How did you know?" she replied in amazement.

"It's a small island.....but I have to confess to making some inquiries. You're so attractive; didn't think I'd be lucky enough find you're unattached. However, on a purely platonic basis, can I buy you a coffee sometime when you're off duty?"

Despina blushed. She was so lonely, and it was such a tempting offer. Surely it wouldn't do any harm. A coffee, after all, was so innocuous.

"Well......I'm not sure," she stuttered. "I'm married......no I can't'" she said with a shake of her head.

"If you change your mind, I'm usually at Costas' place in the afternoon.....looking for inspiration and.....thinking."

Despina walked home in the afternoon carefully avoiding Costas' café and lay on the bed thinking of the handsome Englishman. Thoughts of his sun-bleached hair, wonderful thighs and sensitive hands kept creeping into her mind. One coffee won't do any harm she convinced herself.

Next day after the lunch trade was over she brushed her hair, renewed her lipstick and set off on shaking legs to Costas' cafe

"I can't believe my luck;" he said as she sat down." I've been hoping against hope that you'd turn up. What would you like to drink? Is that seat OK for you? Oh, I'm blabbering like a schoolboy on his first date.........you have that effect on me."

Despina perched nervously on the edge of the chair

and asked for a soft drink.

"Oh, look at the time.......I must go. I'll be late for the evening at the taverna." She picked up her bag and hurried away.

"I'm here every day," she heard Roger's voice follow her down the street.

He's so easy to talk to, she thought. *I can't believe we have chatted for almost two hours. I mustn't do that again* but the next day and the next her feet took her seemingly of their own volition to the same café.

One day Roger tentatively put his hand over hers. His touch sent electric shocks through her body. Feelings that she hadn't thought about for months surged to the surface.

"Despina, you must know how I feel about you.......I can't stand being so close and not able to touch you.......please.....come back to my apartment........let me love you as you should be loved."

"I can't," she gasped in horror. "I'm married."

"But you're not happy."

He took her hand and she allowed herself to be led along a narrow street. It was siesta time and there was no one about. He drew her into an alcove, turned her back to the wall and lowered his lips onto hers.

Despina felt the hot stone on her back, Roger's lips firm and demanding on hers and his body pressing against her urgently. She relaxed into his arms and as he felt her acquiescence his tongue pressed gently on her lips. Despina's lips parted and Roger's tongue explored her mouth. His hands crept up to her breast and she leaned into him feeling a surge of hot longing that she could barely control. Her legs parted as his hand pushed between them.

Suddenly she heard footsteps and pushed Roger away.

What am I doing, she thought desperately. *I'm behaving like a common whore.*

"I'm sorry.....I'm sorry" she sobbed and turned and ran off.

In the silence of her bedroom she watched the fan above the bed and felt the longing for Roger surge through her body again.

"Oh, what'll I do", she whimpered to herself. "I want him so much."

After a long cool shower, she dressed and made her way to the taverna for the evening opening. As she got nearer, she saw a crowd of people. An ambulance siren started wailing and as the crowd parted to let it through, there on the ground lay Giorgos.

"Giorgo what happened?" she cried, all thoughts of Roger banished.

"He got hit by a car,"

. "Just ran into the road......"

"......driver didn't have a chance....."

Despina watched as Giorgos was carefully lifted into the ambulance then she scrambled in with him.

All the way to the hospital, she clutched his hand.

Please be all right, she breathed; not daring to think of the alternative.

She followed the trolley through the hospital corridors as if in a nightmare.

It was late in the evening before Giorgos was settled

in a ward, his leg in plaster and strung up on a pulley.

He looked so pale as she sat by the bed holding his hand.

His eyes opened.

“Despina, I was looking for you .....you were late....you’re never late....I was so worried.....where were you?” he whispered groggily.

“It’s OK....sh.... I’m here now. Get some sleep and get better. The doctor says you’ll be all right. You’ve got a badly broken leg.....you’ll be in for a few days then on crutches for some time after you get out.”

“The café,” he breathed.

“Don’t worry, I’ll sort it out.”

Despina appeared at the café at six the next morning and set about sorting things out. It was a completely different clientele to the taverna.

The retired Greek men were there every morning enjoying their wine, mezzes and games of backgammon; sometimes just reminiscing and exchanging memories; days of sponge fishing, of times when they were virile young men and of businesses come and gone.

She saw Manos the director of the music festival deep in conversation with the very pretty English girl who apparently had won a competition to sing in the festival and by all accounts was very good. Their body language inferred that they were more than friends.

Well, that's fascinating she thought as she watched them sharing some sort of secret joke as they sipped their morning frappes.

In the afternoon when the taverna had closed she went back to check on the café.

Yannis from the bike hire place was there with his lady friend. She was so pleased for him as he had been devastated when his wife left him for a rich businessman from Athens. It seemed he only came alive when his daughter came to the island. But now he was back to his old self and it gladdened her heart to see it.

The girls who served in the cafe were hard workers but needed some direction and as she realised she couldn't be in two places at once she called her sister.

"Maria how would you like a job looking after the café? We could share the time for now......when Giorgos comes out of hospital, he can do mornings and evenings"

It ran like clockwork. Maria enjoyed the challenge and the girls responded to her firm but fair direction.

The ambulance brought Giorgos home tired and pale. He hoisted himself shakily onto his crutches.

"I have to go to the café," were his first words.

"No......." said Despina firmly. "The café's fine. Now...... lie down. It's siesta time."

She made him comfortable on the bed, shut the shutters and turned on the fan.

"Now Giorgo you're going to do as you are told until that leg heals and the first thing we do is have our siesta time again."

"But the café...."

"Maria has everything under control.......and another thing......she's going to run it during the day.....you can do the evening shift."

He looked at Despina in amazement.

"You realise that café almost killed our marriage, well I've arranged it so that we have time for each other again."

She thought.....*if it hadn't been for your accident, I would have made love to Roger. Just in time my darling.*

She lay beside him and heard his relaxed breathing as he slept.

And another thing, she thought, as soon as you are able we are having our afternoon loving. Nothing is going to come between us again.

*****

"You know that I usually like all my guests . . . they're here on holiday, here to enjoy the place and I love telling them about our beautiful island. . . .helping them make the most of things . . . putting some business the way of my friends . . . like Yannis and his bike hire . . . Giorgos and Despina's taverna . . . .telling them to see the interior . . . that we're not all beaches and swimming . . . that there are lush forests and farms . . . . but there was one man I couldn't take to. He was on honeymoon and his wife was a sweetie but there was something about him . . . . "

No more to feel the joy of true romance
That feeling that I thought we'd always have
For you have gone without a backward glance

With love again my eyes will never dance
You cruelly tricked my most innocent of hearts
No more to feel the joy of true romance

We met it seemed by just a lucky chance
You came into my life and changed it all
But you have gone without a backward glance

No more to feel the joy of true romance
But I am stronger than you ever thought
I will think twice before again I'm caught
For you have gone without a backward glance

The Honeymoon

She watched through half closed eyes as John's orange snorkel cut through the crystal clear water of the Aegean Sea.

A smile played over her lips as she listened to the background sounds of the island; the clanging of the goat bells, the insistent chorus of the cicadas and the slap of halyard on mast. The faint scent of sage was in the air and the warm sun caressed her skin.

I'm in heaven, she thought, I'm so lucky.

I can't believe that last year all I cared about was my job.

She was the manager of a large accounting practice; she was smart, efficient and clever.

Mathematics had always been her subject and she had no difficulty at school in mastering the intricacies of the subject and enjoyed the challenge and the symmetry of numbers. Accountancy had been an obvious choice of career and she had sailed through without much effort before landing a position with an illustrious accounting firm and her competence on the technical side and sympathetic handling of the clients had eased her rise to the manager.

She had been a woman in a man's world.

She stuck rigidly to the rules in the book 'Dress for Success' *(MALLOY, J. T., The Woman's Dress for Success. Warner Books, 1978)* and never allowed herself to relax them.

She felt she had always to appear smart, efficient and completely non-sexual. Her wardrobe consisted of tailored suits, shirt-blouses and sensible court shoes. Her long dark hair was at all times pulled back quite severely and she wore a minimum of make-up. She never even approached the maximum recommended amount of five pieces of jewellery. She only ever wore a very practical wrist watch and a pair of unobtrusive gold earrings; only a briefcase was carried; never a handbag. However, she did keep a small clutch in her office drawer in case she wanted to meet someone for lunch; not that that was a regular occurrence as her job didn't leave her much time for socialising and she was a very reserved and private person anyway.

Sadly her parents died within a few months of each other and as an only child she inherited the house. A substantial Victorian detached house it sat in its own small garden in the suburbs. Her mother had owned a fair amount of gold jewellery showered on her by her adoring husband and that fell to Anne as well. Since she had no rent or mortgage and a substantial salary she treated herself to an expensive German car. Her life was satisfying, her job challenging but if she was honest she was sometimes a tiny bit lonely.

John came to the office for tax advice. After going through all his paperwork she asked him to come back with more information. This was unusual as she normally would have had a client call her or mail her the requisite papers but for some reason she felt she would like to see him again.

On the day of his appointment, she took more care than usual with her appearance and even changed to a slightly darker shade of lipstick. She rationalised her behaviour with the thought that every client deserves her best shot.

This was her last appointment of the day but after

the business part of the meeting was concluded successfully she could think of no reason to detain him further but then to her surprise, he hesitantly asked if she would like to have a coffee with him.

He was slim and unassuming with floppy brown hair that fell endearingly over his forehead. When the conversation turned to work he told Anne that he was in the Civil Service; a boring office job. He wore smart but casual clothes, usually slacks and a blazer. A quiet and self-deprecating sense of humour attracted her and although no Adonis he was thoughtful and charming.

Coffee led to a dinner date.

Smiling she remembered how she'd panicked at the thought of what to wear. Her wardrobe held nothing suitable so she'd gone on a shopping spree. She treated herself to a soft A-line skirt in dark brown and a cashmere sweater in a soft green that set off her dark hair and slightly olive skin. The evening of the date she had dressed with care, applied makeup carefully and sprayed Chanel on wrists and neck. Some carefully chosen pieces of her mother's jewellery finished the outfit.

. He had taken a step back as she opened the door, "Oh......gosh....you look.... beautiful."

She had actually blushed; had felt her cheeks burn; a completely new sensation.

"I thought we'd go in my car so you can have a glass of wine," he said and again Anne thought how very considerate he was.

The dinner was perfect; the conversation effortless and the evening flew. To her disappointment, he had kissed her cheek at the door and left.

What was I expecting, she thought. I was so naïve.

Did I expect him to sweep me into his arms on the first date? Methinks I read too many romantic novels.

However, one date led to another and one time he accepted the invite inside. As she bustled around the kitchen she wondered how she could encourage him. As she handed him the mug of coffee their hands brushed. He had looked up shyly.

"Would you mind terribly if.....if I kissed you?" he stuttered. She laid the mugs back down on the counter and stepped his arms. His lips were warm and soft. Tentatively his hand crept up to her breast and her knees turned to water.

Although not a virgin her sexual experiences were quite limited but she knew that she wanted this very badly. She wanted this quiet sensitive man to make love to her. She had this idea that they could learn together how to make this a wonderful experience.

'Do you mind?' he whispered.

She had replied by taking his hand and leading him to the bedroom; coffee abandoned and forgotten.

He surprised her by turning out to be a considerate lover. He took time to ensure her needs were satisfied. He showed her pleasures she had never even dreamt existed. It fleetingly crossed her mind to wonder how he knew exactly what to do to satisfy her so expertly but she quickly brushed the thoughts aside. They lay side by side afterwards sated and relaxed.

That's when I changed, she thought.

Her job became secondary; her dress habits changed; softer more feminine clothes filled her wardrobe, she experimented with makeup and wore more than the five pieces of jewellery as laid down in 'Dress for Success'. All she wanted was to please John and nothing was too much trouble or too expensive for him. She couldn't wait for him to call, couldn't wait for his kiss and ultimately to end up in bed.

Before long it seemed the natural sequence of events for John to move in and she remembered her delight when he proposed.

He had come home one evening with a bottle of champagne.

“I'll cook dinner tonight, my darling. You go and soak in a bath and get rid of all thoughts of boring accountancy and all will be ready when you come back down.”

She reappeared to see the dining room table beautifully set with all her best china and cutlery. There was a wonderful smell emanating from the kitchen and John was opening the champagne and pouring it into her crystal flutes.

He handed her a glass then laid his down on the table.

“Before we start to eat my darling, I have something to ask you.”

To Anne's amazement he dropped to one knee and took her hand.

“Will you make me the happiest man in the world and marry me?”

Tears welled.

“I can't believe this . . . . of course I'll marry you,” she sobbed happily.

The evening progressed perfectly almost like a romantic movie. They drank the champagne, demolished a perfectly cooked meal then finished a bottle of good red wine.

Slightly squiffy they made their way to the bedroom where John excelled himself in his lovemaking.

The wedding was a quiet affair; only two of her friends as witnesses. John's parents were dead and he had no siblings.

Now I'm on my honeymoon; I'm lying on a beach on a Greek island watching my new husband snorkel. I love the word – husband, she hugged the thought to herself.

They had arrived on this little Greek island a few days previously and checked into the one hotel. It was a gem of a place around the point from the main harbour. The owner, bartender and general factotum was Manolis. This man was a fount of information about the island and the facilities thereon.

Under his guidance, they had hired a scooter from Yannis at the bike hire kiosk and explored the road through the middle of the island. It was a hair-raising journey along roads with a sheer drop at the side and no protective barriers. However, the views were amazing and when they arrived at the monastery at the southern tip the atmosphere was so tranquil. Anne was not really of a religious persuasion but in the small but ornate Greek Orthodox Church she felt peace seep into her very soul. They lit candles and carefully placed them in the tray of sand and felt completely in harmony with the surroundings.

On the way back they stopped at a small stony beach where the water sparkled in the sun and they swam before lunching at a quintessentially Greek taverna. There were geraniums spilling out of a variety of containers and tins, a few cats dozing in shady spots and Grandma doing all the cooking and producing the most wonderful dolmades with Greek salad washed down by icy cold retsina.

On another day they took a trip around the island. They swam off the boat in deserted coves. Anne admired John's prowess as he dived off the back of the boat but she was not so brave and lowered herself demurely down the ladders. The barbeque served up at lunchtime was a veritable feast and it was difficult to believe it had all been freshly prepared in the tiny galley kitchen. They arrived back at the hotel tired, happy and streaked with salt from the saline water of the Aegean.

"I told you it's a magical day out," said Manolis as they passed him in reception.

"No better way to see the island,"

Each evening after a shower and freshen up they would have a pre-dinner drink with Manolis then wander around the harbour to eat at whatever taverna took their fancy.

Sometimes they went for cheap and cheerful amazingly tasty Greek food. One night for a special treat they went to a restaurant that only served a selection of mezzes. These are starter size plates. The challenge was to see how many you can get through before you feel you can't eat another mouthful.

Anne thought it was going to be a blast as she confidently attacked a salad, salmon wrapped in filo pastry, shrimps in cheese sauce, tiny slices of lamb with rosemary, a small slice of moussaka but when it came to a child size portion of curry she was having difficulty facing another mouthful of delicious food. She gave in gracefully and watched as John downed a small beef stifado and a slice of goat before he threw in the towel as well. They laughed as the waiter presented them with complimentary desserts as they felt stuffed to the gunnels but managed to clear up the panacotta and lemon mousse washed down by crisp local wine.

The previous evening they had gone to a musical recital in the church courtyard and heard a young girl with a most amazing voice. The setting was enchanting. The churchyard had flooring of blue and white pebbled mosaic. It was shielded by several tall black cypress trees that reached up to a navy blue sky studded with a panoply of stars. The blazing heat of the day had softened to the velvet warmth of the evening. They walked back to the hotel hand in hand quietly contemplating the musical feast they had heard.

As today was their second last day they had decided to stay on the local beach just around the point from the hotel.

Anne opened her eyes again but there was no sign of the orange snorkel

Obviously got carried away and gone round the rocks. She shut her eyes again and gave her senses up to the wonders of Greece.

People were packing up and leaving the beach to shower and change before dinner but still no sign of John. Restlessly she scanned the water but nothing.

What to do? She was alone on the beach. By 6 o'clock she had packed up the accoutrements of the day but didn't quite know what to do next.

Suddenly she thought, I expect he's gone back to the hotel and is waiting for me. He probably swam around the cove and it was easier to walk back.

Feeling heartened she picked up the bag and headed along the path.

She opened the room door and although there was no

sign of John she knew he had been there.

One of the new matching set of suitcases had gone, his side of the wardrobe had been emptied and when she checked the mini safe his passport had gone.

“Has my husband checked out?” she asked hesitantly. The handset was slippery in her shaking palm.

"Yes Ma'am, he had to go back suddenly but said you would be staying until tomorrow as planned," Manolis answered feeling desperately sorry for the new bride.

She tossed and turned in the big double bed. John’s mobile was turned off. She tried the house ‘phone but only the answering machine clicked in. What could have happened; why hadn’t he got in touch? At three am she was pacing the floor.

The flight home was a nightmare. The charter plane was packed; it was delayed by four hours and then seemed full of drunken noisy young men. Considering she had no sleep the night before it was almost more than she could bear.

Wearily she trundled her suitcase out of arrivals and caught the shuttle bus to the car park.

Where John had parked the car there was only an empty space. Lying in the dirt was the plastic heart that had dangled from the rear-view mirror.

There had been a fair in the local park and they had gone along one evening. Anne remembered how John had helped her hold the rifle at the shooting stall while kissing her ear, they laughed as they ate candy floss and it stuck to their noses and cheeks. At the final stall, Anne had managed to score three ducks in a row and won the plastic heart. They had joked that it was a symbol of their love and now it was discarded in the dust.

The police took notes but didn't give out much hope.

She paid the taxi and opened the front door. The house was empty but the faint whiff of the aftershave that John favoured told her he had been and gone.

Her case bumped up each step and as she swung it up onto the bed she saw her jewellery case was open; Mother's gold had gone!

On impulse, she booted up the computer and logged into their joint bank account – empty!

She could hardly breathe as the sobs wracked her body. The policewoman tried to encourage her to drink the tea that was cooling on the pitted table. The room was drab; no windows; walls an institutional green; smelling of stale smoke and sweat. Her head dropped hopelessly onto her hands and she wanted to die.

"Now..... Mrs Brown, I know this is difficult.....but please......look at this..... is this your husband?"

She opened her swollen eyelids and there in the photo, smiling his charming smile, hair flopping captivatingly over his forehead was John.

"That's him; that's my husband; what's happened?"

"Mrs Brown, I'm so sorry......there's no way to break this gently ...but.... this man's a serial bigamist. He's 'so-called' married several women and then cleaned them out of their assets. He always chooses women like you; no family connections, well-paid job and dare I say it, past the first flush of youth..... now......you're the first real lead. You can help us so that he doesn't do to any more women what he has done to you and the others."

Her head throbbed to bursting point. Faint and dizzy with crying she felt a sudden need to relieve her bladder.

"May I use the ladies?" she choked between

shuddering sobs.

She came out of the cubicle and turned on the tap to wash her hands. A strange face looked back from the mirror. She looked exactly what she was – a dupe. Hair hanging in rats' tails, eyes were swollen almost shut and cheeks red and blotchy; her body language shrieked victim. The trousers and sweater that she had travelled in were crumpled and grubby.

Where was the super-efficient career woman, the woman who confidently managed a large office, the woman who coped with the intricacies of accounting and tax; the woman who had dressed for success and succeeded.

I've become the sort of woman I've always despised, she thought with sudden clarity. I've become a woman totally dependent on a man; a woman whose whole being is wrapped up in his approval; surely that's not what relationships are about. I've been such a fool.

She dug into her handbag and found a comb and a clip. She tugged the comb through her tangled hair, swept it up into the usual chignon and clipped it in place. She leaned over the wash basin and splashed and splashed icy water on her face until it was stinging and cold.

Not perfect, she thought looking back in the mirror but it's a start. Her eyes were hard and clear.

Head high she strode back into the interview room.

"Right, I'll tell you everything I can think of. Now...... let's catch the bastard....."

*****

"Did you ever find out what happened? . . . That poor woman . . . "

“I’ll never forget the day he sneaked back into the hotel, dripping wet and in his swimming gear. He thought I hadn’t seen him. About half an hour later he appeared at reception with his suitcase and told me he was checking out as he had to go back on urgent business and would I tell his wife to stick to the original plan and fly back the next day . . . . she arrived from the beach sometime after six o’clock . . . .I presume she had been waiting for him to appear . . . .then she called reception to ask if her husband had checked out . . . . what could I say . . . she was obviously upset.”

"So she flew home the next day . . . Oh, how I would love to hear the end of the story."

"Well . . . funnily enough, I have a friend who works in the courts in London and he told me of a case that came before the court, a case of bigamy... .the name was John Brown . . . . I can't be sure... but I would dearly like to think it was him . . . if it was he was convicted and jailed which proves there is some justice . . ."

“So my friend . . . you’ve had a good season, met interesting people and are you opening in the winter?”

"Well, I'm considering having a couple of rooms available to see if there is any winter trade. The problem in the winter is the ferries. If there's bad weather there can be days of delays and that's no good if you have a flight to catch . . . but we'll see . . . .I'll give it a try."

“And tell m.... how’s the family?”

“They’re all well. Mona’s pleased that the season is drawing to a close as she can have a day off . . . .her legs are bothering her . . . . we’re not getting any younger. Haris loves the hotel and he will take over more and more of my work as time goes on and Irini is still living in the UK with her British husband. She’s very happy there and I'm hoping that she will give me a grandchild sometime in the near future. We have to look to the next generation now my friend as you well know."

"Am I right in thinking that tomorrow is the big name day at the church in the bay?"

"Yes . . . I think most of us are going. We reckon we can have a morning off. I hope you'll join us, my friend. It's many years since we have seen you at a name day. The taxi boat leaves the harbour at seven thirty."

So here I am; up, showered, dressed and walking to the harbour in the early morning sun; an unearthly hour but really the best time of day. Although it's already October the day promises to be very hot.

The harbour is quiet with that hush, like a holding of breath that precedes the start of a busy summer day on a Greek island; yawning taverna owners are sweeping up the previous evening's detritus and setting out the tables and chairs in readiness for the day's onslaught of tourists. Tablecloths are being smoothed; painted upright chairs positioned meticulously; ready to accommodate the bottoms of hungry tourists.

On the way, I see Yannis and Maria, Manos and Sophie among other familiar faces.

As promised, the boat is waiting and we board and sit with a group of ladies dressed in their best black and carrying an assortment of icons, flowers and religious pictures. We all exchange a polite *kalimera* then fall silent as the boat busily chugs its way through the still water, out of the harbour and around the bay.

The water is like a mill pond. I look down and let my hand drag in the cool liquid. It is amazingly clear. I can see the fish and the rocky bottom; my face is reflected in its surface as if in a rippling mirror. I think once again how lucky I am to live in such a paradise and how silly I was to have spent so much time away.

By the time we disembark and climb up the steep steps to the small church the perspiration is running down my back. I find a shady spot in the courtyard and sink down thankfully. I rummage in my pocket for a handkerchief and dab ineffectually at the perspiration beading on my face and neck. My shorts and shirt, so fresh when I left the house, stick to my skin like damp rags.

Recovering my composure I look around. The majority of the congregation sit out in the courtyard. People are chatting, catching up on gossip and, it seems they are completely ignoring the service. It wasn't like this when I was a small boy and had to listen quietly to the Papa. Chanting emanates from the dark interior of the tiny whitewashed church. It is strangely soporific. The churchyard is shaded by thick, dark green trees. They stretch upwards drawing the eye up to a large expanse of brittle blue sky. The building has obviously been recently redecorated and the newly whitewashed walls reflect the blindingly bright sun.

Then a lone cicada hidden deep in the heart of a tall cypress tree, begins to chirrup. This is a sound I always associate with hot island summers. It is gradually joined by others until the chorus is insistent and deafening. The louder the chanting from the church, the louder it seems the cicadas become as if trying to outdo the human sounds invading their territory. Then suddenly, as if an unseen orchestral conductor has dropped his baton, the chirruping stops. The silence is palpable then once again only the soft voice of the chanter fills the hot still air.

The sudden loud and happy tolling of the bells jerks

me out of my reverie.

The Papa appears wearing the most beautiful robes. He sweeps round carrying the incense, shaking it liberally over us. The heavy scent fills my nostrils as it filters through the air and droplets land on my skin and clothes. As he comes from the shade into a patch of sun the gold embroidery that encrusts the robe and high mitred hat glitters and sparkles like a thousand golden stars. He stops at a trestle table that holds several loaves of round dark bread carefully placed on a spotless heavily embroidered white cloth. The bread is blessed at some length and with great ceremony. It is then broken, placed in a basket and we each receive a precious slice. It has an interesting aniseed flavour and my senses seem bombarded with the tastes, scents, sounds, feel and sights happening all around me.

The food and drink begin to appear. Tiny cups of incredibly sweet coffee, small boxes of orange juice and bottles of refrigerated water; doughnuts dripping with Greek honey, homemade cakes and sugary biscuits are being passed around and pressed upon us. A plastic bag is provided in order to carry away the goodies that are surplus to immediate requirements.

Afterwards, Manolis and I wander down to the beach. I strip down to my swimming shorts and slip into the sea. I feel the cool silky water caress my hot skin. I swim for a bit then turn on my back. The buoyant salty water supports my weight as if I am floating on a giant water bed.

I can hear the muted sound of voices from the beach overlaid by the slow clang clang of the goat bells from the mountain. I open my eyes and squint up at the intense sapphire blue of the cloudless sky and watch a lone seagull drifting lazily. The white trail of a jet carrying intrepid travellers miles above the earth steadily traverses my field of vision. A boat potters its way along the other side of the bay sending out gentle waves that rock me tenderly in its wake.

For lunch, we find a private spot in the shade and eat the cakes and biscuits given to us at the church washed down by icy cold water – delicious!

Another swim in the heavenly water then it is time to go home.

The regular taxi boat takes us back to the harbour. We are hot and tired and our skin is white with crystallised sea salt.

The harbour is bustling as we get off the boat. The tavernas are full of holidaymakers enjoying a late lunch or sipping cold beer out of iced glasses while people watching. A constant stream of folks stroll by; there are scantily dressed young girls; parents dragging hot, whining and tired children; young men with bare chests posing in groups trying to look macho. People are people wherever you are. From time immemorial girls have giggled in clusters while eyeing up the boys and the boys have strutted and postured hoping to be noticed by one of them.

Wearily we retrace our steps of the morning, heading for the shower, fresh clothes and the evening meal.

I wonder why I left this paradise and am pleased and grateful to be back.

*****

Acknowledgements

Thank you to Michael Terence Publishing for encouraging me to publish then leading me patiently through the process and helping me overcome various technical hitches.

Thank you to the Dutch artist Cobi Sanders for supplying the beautiful illustrations. You can see more of her work on her website www.cobisanders.gr

Finally, thank you to my husband for his unwavering support and for always being there for me.

About Patricia Frew

Patricia is a retired accountant. Born and brought up in Scotland but has lived and worked in Canada, the Caribbean and the South East of England.

She has one daughter and two grandchildren.

On retirement, she decided to try something completely different and undertook a course in creative writing.

Short stories have brought her some success but this is her first novel.

In the winter months she loves to travel but in the summer she can be found enjoying the hot weather in Greece where she now lives with her husband.

28161399R00059

Printed in Great Britain
by Amazon